STERLING CHILDREN'S BOOKS
New York

An Imprint of Sterling Publishing
1166 Avenue of the Americas
New York, NY 10036

ISBN 978-1-4549-1698-7

Distributed in Canada by Sterling Publishing
c/o Canadian Manda Group, 664 Annette Street
Toronto, Ontario, Canada M6S 2C8.
Distributed in the United Kingdom by GMC Distribution Services
Castle Place, 166 High Street, Lewes, East Sussex, England BN7 1XU
Distributed in Australia by Capricorn Link (Australia) Pty. Ltd.
P.O. Box 704, Windsor, NSW 2756, Australia

For information about custom editions, special sales, and premium and corporate purchases,
please contact Sterling Special Sales at 800-805-5489 or specialsales@sterlingpublishing.com.

Designed by Andrea Miller

Manufactured in China
Lot #:
2 4 6 8 10 9 7 5 3 1
03/16

www.sterlingpublishing.com

To Mom, who can't predict the future but knows that the sun will come out.—K.A.

To my dear friends and family, who were able to tell the future when I couldn't.—L.M.

MIRA
FORECASTS
THE
FUTURE

by Kell Andrews · illustrated by Lissy Marlin

STERLING CHILDREN'S BOOKS
New York

Mira couldn't tell the future. That wouldn't bother most people in town,
who lived their lives front-ways forwards with few surprises along the way.
But Mira wasn't most people.

She was the daughter of Famous Madame Mirabella, the Miracle by the Sea.
Folks came from all over to hear their futures.

When Madame gazed into the
crystal ball, it swirled with magic.

When Mira gazed into it, she saw herself . . . only a bit different.

But she tried to tell fortunes anyway.

"Something big is coming your way."

"Good luck will fall in your lap."

"You will enjoy attention from a flock of admirers."

Even when she was right, she was wrong.

"Telling the future is a gift," Madame said.
"You have it, or you don't."

Mira didn't.

"You're good at lots of other things," Madame said.
"Like helping me."
All Mira had to do was predict the wait time.
But she wasn't even good at that.

Waiting
Time
1 5
Minutes

Each day during summer,
Mira watched the boardwalk
while her mother peered into palms.

One morning Madame clipped a pinwheel and a windsock next to Mira's chair.
"I saw you looking at them," said Mira's mom.

The next morning, Fred the fisherman came over.

"What's your prediction, Mira?" asked Fred the fisherman.
"Will it be nice enough to fish all morning?"

Mira was about to say she couldn't predict the future. But then . . .

She saw the wind gently whirring the blades of her pinwheel and fluttering the streamers on her windsock. She felt the warm air and the hot sun on her skin. She studied the clouds that were whiter and fluffier than cotton candy.

"It'll be sunny all morning," she said. "You can fish as long as you want, but it's up to the fish to bite."

At lunchtime, Fred came back. "You were right, Mira. So what weather is headed our way?"

"Ask again tomorrow," she said. "I'll let you know."

At the library that evening, Mira and Madame found books about weather.

Mira figured out just what to do.

Thermometer: The thermometer measures the temperature. It tells us how hot or cold it is.

Barometer: It doesn't feel like air has weight, but it does! The barometer measures how much the air is pressing on the earth. When air pressure is high, skies are usually sunny. When air pressure is low, skies are usually cloudy.

Rain Gauge: A rain gauge measures precipitation, like rain and snow. A jar with measurements on the side can be used as a rain gauge. The water collects in the jar so it can be measured.

Windsock: You can't see the wind, but you can definitely feel it! Windsocks show which way the wind is blowing.

Anemometer: An anemometer measures the wind speed. A pinwheel is like an anemometer because when the wind blows hard, the pinwheel spins faster.

Clouds: There are two main kinds: cumulus, which are puffy, and stratus, which are flat and layered. Clouds are made of tiny water drops. When they are gray, they are full of water and more likely to rain.

On the way home, they stopped at the
hardware store for supplies. Mira painted,
twisted, hooked, and glued until bedtime.

In the morning, Mira opened for business.

"What's your prediction?" Fred asked.
Mira read the temperature on her thermometer and the air pressure on her barometer. She checked her windsock and pinwheel for the direction and speed of the wind. She observed the color of the sky and the shape of the clouds. "Overcast this morning. Clear in the afternoon," Mira said.

She was right. Word spread.

"What's your prediction?"
asked Taylor the lifeguard.
"Sunny. Wear SPF 100," Mira said.

"What's your prediction?"
asked Mrs. O'Mooney the shopkeeper.
"Rainy. Keep the postcards inside," Mira said.

"What's your prediction?"
asked Sal the pizza maker.
"Hot. Make extra lemonade," she said.

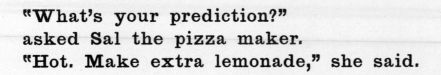

Mira was usually right:

sunshine,

wind,

and rainstorms.

And sometimes wrong.

"Not even Madame Mirabella is right all the time," said her mom.

The day of the annual surf competition came.

Beachgoers came from all over the state to see surfers from all over the world.
It was the busiest day on the boardwalk with the whole town counting on sunshine.

"What's your prediction, Mira? Good weather for the surf contest today?" asked Taylor the lifeguard. Mira checked the thermometer and wind gauge. She read the barometer.

The sky was blue, and there was not a cloud in sight.

"I predict," Mira said, "sunny through morning."

The contest was underway.

Surfers rode the waves.

Tourists crowded the beach.

Then Mira checked her gauges.
The barometer reading had dropped.
Dark clouds were rolling in.

She ran to the lifeguard stand.
"Taylor, a storm is coming!" she shouted.
"Get everyone off the beach!"

Taylor the lifeguard ran to the celebrity judge, but he wouldn't listen. "The sun is still shining," said the judge. "The girl could be wrong."

"Mira's usually right," said Fred the fisherman.
"She's just a kid," said the celebrity judge.
"She knows what she's doing," said Mrs. O'Mooney the shopkeeper.
"It's too important to cancel," said the celebrity judge.
"It's too dangerous to risk," said Mira's mom.

"Listen to Mira!" said Madame.
"Listen to Mira!" said Sal the pizza maker.
"Listen to Mira!" said Taylor the lifeguard.

The celebrity judge finally nodded.

Taylor the lifeguard blew her whistle. Surfers coasted out of the water. Tourists flip-flopped into the boardwalk shops and waited.

And waited.

The day turned dark as night.

Water poured from the sky.

Lightning lit up the ocean.

Waves pounded the sand where sunbathers had lounged and children had played.
The boardwalk shook with the crash of thunder.

Outside a storm raged. Inside the boardwalk shops, the surfers, beachgoers, shopkeepers, and Mira huddled safe and dry. "Mira, you saved us," a surfer said.

Madame hugged her.
"Telling the future is a gift for me," she said. "For you, it's a science."

Mira smiled.
She had told the future after all.

She predicted that the next day, she'd do it again.

As usual, she was right.